Jungle Trek

by Stephanie St. Pierre
illustrated by George Ulrich

SCHOLASTIC INC.
New York Toronto London Auckland Sydney

Based on the TV Series *Rugrats*® created by Klasky/Csupo Inc. and Paul Germain
as seen on Nickelodeon®

ISBN 0-590-63444-5

12 11 10 9 8 7   9/9 0 1 2 3/0

Printed in the U.S.A.   23

First Scholastic printing, September 1998

It was a hot summer afternoon and the babies were getting restless.

"What are you babies doing?" asked Angelica.

"We're making a big pile of sand," said Tommy.

"Do you wanna help?" Phil and Lil asked. Angelica made a face and walked away.

"I'm going to do something much more interesting than *that*," she said.

Angelica put on a big straw hat. Tommy, Phil, and Lil watched from the sandbox. Next, Angelica put on a vest with lots and lots of pockets.

"What's she gonna do?" wondered Tommy.

"She's putting cookies in her pockets," said Phil.

"And juice boxes!" added Lil.

All three babies climbed out of the sandbox and crawled over to get a closer look at Angelica. Her pockets were bulging but she kept packing them with more stuff.

"What are you staring at?" Angelica asked as she finished filling her pockets.

"Hmm, I wonder if I should tell you about my expedition. Maybe I better not. I don't think it's the kind of thing babies like you would understand."

"Tell us, *please*," begged Phil and Lil.

"Okay," Angelica said, "but if I do, promise you won't get in my way."

"We won't," Phil and Lil and Tommy promised.

"Or be scared of stuff and cry," Angelica said.

"We won't," the babies promised again.

"If I tell you," Angelica began, "and you come along, you have to do *everything* I say, because this expedition could be dangerous."

"What's an expedition, Angelica?" asked Tommy.

"A jungle trek, that's what," said Angelica. "Do you think you can handle that?" She stared hard at Tommy and Phil and Lil.

They nodded nervously.

Soon Tommy and Phil and Lil were loaded up with gear. Angelica found a backpack for each baby and filled it up with snacks and maps. She brought a hat for everyone, even Spike.

"Spike can come with us," said Angelica. "To protect us from the wild animals." The babies gulped. "Is everybody ready?"

They plunged into the thick green branches and began their trek through the jungle. Spike ran ahead of them, sniffing.

"Do you think he smells an aminal?" Lil asked Tommy. It was kind of dark in the jungle. There were lots of scratchy branches and strange shapes.

"Maybe he's found a cropodile," said Angelica. "Or a big snake. Or even a panther. You better stick close to me or who knows what might happen." Phil and Lil and Tommy were getting scared. They huddled together.

"Remember, you promised not to cry," said Angelica. "Let's get moving." But now the babies were too scared to go any further.

"Come on, you dumb babies!" cried Angelica. She was getting impatient with this trip through the jungle. It wasn't turning out the way she had expected.

Suddenly Angelica screamed, "Ahhhh!"

"What's the matter, Angelica?" asked Tommy. "You aren't scared of a little spider, are you?" He reached toward the thread that the tiny spider was hanging from and pinched it between his fingers. He moved the thread away from Angelica, and the spider dropped onto a leaf and disappeared. "It's so eensie-weensie."

"I wasn't scared," said Angelica. She shivered.

"All right, what's everybody looking at?" said Angelica, regaining her composure. "We'll see how all of you hold up when we cross that mountain!"

"Uh-oh," said Phil and Lil.

"Come on, guys," said Tommy. "We can do it."

They trudged along after Angelica to the foot of the mountain.

The babies started up the mountain. Getting to the top wasn't easy. Spike took the lead and disappeared over the top.

"Looks like Spike found a trail," said Tommy.

"I wouldn't try to follow him," said Angelica, who was peering over the top. "There are snakes down there."

"Hey, we made it," said Tommy. He stood at the top of the mountain and looked around.

"Whoa!" Before he knew it, he was sliding down the side of the mountain. Angelica, Phil, and Lil followed close behind.

They landed—thump, thump, thump, thump—one after the other in the hot sandy desert.

"Ugh, I got sand in my mouth," said Lil. "I need some juice."

"No snacks until we cross that desert, babies," said Angelica. "Now, crawl before this sun dries us up like raisins."

They all crawled forward through the hot sand. Only the thought of juice and cookies on the other side kept them going.

Finally they reached the shade of the cool, green jungle. After all the excitement, everyone needed cookies and juice.

"There's nothing like a cookie after surviving a dangerous abenture," said Phil.

Suddenly Tommy asked, "Where's Spike?" They strained to see through the thick leaves. "I hope the snakes didn't get him."

"There he is!" said Phil. Spike was busy digging.

Tommy gasped. "Look! Spike's found something!"

"Wow!" said Phil and Lil together. "Maybe it's a treasure!"

"Yeah, treasure like some smelly old sock," said Angelica.

"Let's help Spike!" said Tommy. They ran over and peered into the hole.

"Everyone, grab hold and pull," Tommy cried. "One, two, three . . . pull!" They pulled as hard as they could. When the treasure came loose, everyone went flying.

"Ouf!" said Tommy as he rolled over Phil and Lil.

"Ouch!" Angelica cried. She had stumbled into a bush.

"We got it!" Phil and Lil shouted. They held the treasure above their heads. Spike jumped up and down and barked.

"But what is it?" asked Tommy.

"Can't you tell?" said Angelica. She reached for the thing and held it on her head. "It's . . . er . . . a crown, of course. Fit for a princess. It looks perfect on me. . . ."

Suddenly a big clump of dirt fell onto Angelica's face.

"Blech," she said and threw it down. "Never mind, it's just an old piece of junk."

"Space junk," said Phil. "Maybe a satakite, you know, those things that fly around in space and send pictures into the TV."

"No, it's pirate junk," said Lil. "This could be all that's left of some terrible pirate ship."

"Maybe it's a dinosaur bone," said Tommy. "Whatever it is, it's cool. Let's take it home!"

"Going home won't be so easy," grumbled Angelica. "We still have to get through this jungle. Anything could happen . . . and probably will." Phil and Lil looked worried.

The babies started back, carrying the mysterious object high above their heads. While Angelica kept a wary eye out for spiders, the Rugrats sang a little jungle-trekking song.

When they returned home, they found their parents preparing lunch.

"Look, Didi," said Stu. He was getting ready to start the barbecue. "The kids are back. What's that thing they're carrying?"

"Gosh, it looks like an old sprinkler," said Didi. "I wonder where it came from?"

Didi attached a hose to the sprinkler.

"Hey, look at that! Water is coming out of the dinosaur bone!" said Tommy with surprise.

"It must be a satakite rain-making thingamajig that fell from the sky!" said Phil.

"No, it's what pirates used to make their enemies walk the plank!" said Lil.

"Oh, you babies don't know anything! It's a crown for an underwater mermaid!"

"Whatever it is, let's play!" The Rugrats happily danced around in the water.